W9-AAE-314

A TALE *of* TULIPS, A TALE *of* ONIONS

A TALE *of* TULIPS, A TALE *of* ONIONS

BY *David Francis Birchman*
ILLUSTRATED BY *Jonathan Hunt*

FOUR WINDS PRESS ✲ *New York*
MAXWELL MACMILLAN CANADA *Toronto* MAXWELL MACMILLAN INTERNATIONAL *New York Oxford Singapore Sydney*

Four Winds Press
Macmillan Publishing Company
866 Third Avenue
New York, NY 10022
Maxwell Macmillan Canada, Inc.
1200 Eglinton Avenue East
Suite 200
Don Mills, Ontario M3C 3N1
Macmillan Publishing Company is part of the Maxwell Communication Group of Companies.
First edition
Printed and bound in the United States of America on recycled paper.

10 9 8 7 6 5 4 3 2 1

The text of this book is set in Bembo.
The illustrations for this book were done in transparent watercolors and acrylics on 140 lb. hot pressed rag paper. The paintings were color separated by laser-scanner and reproduced in four colors using magenta, cyan, yellow, and black inks.
Book design by Christy Hale

Library of Congress Cataloging-in-Publication Data
Birchman, David Francis.
A tale of tulips, a tale of onions / by David Birchman ; illustrated by Jonathan Hunt.—1st ed.
p. cm.
Summary: Amid the tulipomania craze in seventeenth-century Holland, gardener Ed Vard Grooter's love of tulips and sea captain Drooter Van Zooter's love of onions almost bring them to blows.
ISBN 0-02-710112-6
[1. Tulips—Fiction. 2. Onions—Fiction. 3. Netherlands—History—Fiction. 4. Humorous stories.] I. Hunt, Jonathan, ill. II. Title.
PZ7.B511877Tal 1994
[Fic]—dc20 92-31240

To my mother, Florine
To my in-laws, Margaret and Lester Turcott
—grandparents all

—D. F. B.

This one is for my grandparents
Jennie & Herbert Hunt and Esther & William Oakley,
who always reminded me to stop and smell the tulips!

—J. H.

THIS IS A TALE OF TULIPS. THIS IS A TALE OF ONIONS.
WE WROTE IT THIS WAY 'CAUSE WE JUST COULDN'T SAY
IF IT WAS TRULY TU TALES OR JUST ONE-IONS.

A TALE *of* TULIPS

Ed Vard Grooter loved tulips—all kinds of tulips: dwarf tulips, parrot-petal tulips, pointy-petaled tulips, petaled pointy tulips, blushing Keizerkroons, and blooming Zomerschoons. Ed Vard Grooter loved his tulips more than anything else in the whole of Holland—except for Gretel Grooter, his darling daughter.

Then one day, Ed Vard Grooter heard about a remarkable tulip growing in another garden, in another part of Holland. It was a white tulip with bizarre purple speckles. Ed Vard Grooter knew at once that this tulip was the most valuable flower in all the world.

"Why, a white tulip with bizarre purple speckles is worth at least a gaggle of ganders and a giggle of geese, eight snorting pigs and twelve shearable sheep," exclaimed Ed Vard Grooter. He moaned with envy. "If only such a tulip grew in my garden!"

A TALE *of* ONIONS

Captain Drooter van Zooter loved onions—all kinds of onions: raggedy-headed round onions, bulbous-bottomed red onions, long, slim leeks, and skinny, limp green onions. Onions hung from the pockets of Captain Drooter van Zooter's vest and pants, and he carried them under his hat.

Gretel Grooter loved Captain Drooter van Zooter, and she loved to cook him onions. She stewed them, she boiled them, she baked them, she fried them—usually with liver and cod.

One day, Meener Horst Hilder, owner of the *Gulden Guilder*, a flute that flew the seven seas (sailing moo cows to the Moluccan Isles and loads of spice to the Zeiderzees), strolled through the door and stared down at Captain Drooter van Zooter, who was sitting at a table heaped with piles and piles of onions.

"Captain Zooter, you're a man of the sea, and that's what I need to sail with a cargo of cats—a spotted, calico, striped, meooowable, purrrrable cargo of cats," Meener Horst Hilder said.

"A cargo of cats! Where does one sail with a cargo of cats?" asked Captain Drooter van Zooter.

"To Kracka-toe-Krack, where we've trouble with rats, that's where you'll go with your cargo of cats," said Meener Horst Hilder. "The rats there are brazen, they're big, and they're mean. They've eaten our peppers, papayas, pineapples, and passion fruit, too. That's why we need you to sail to Kracka-toe-Krack with a cargo of cats."

Captain Drooter van Zooter stared up at Gretel Grooter and then at his table heaped with piles and piles of onions. "Yes, I'll go to Kracka-toe-Krack with a cargo of cats," he finally replied, "provided I can take my onions."

A TALE *of* TULIPS

While working in his garden that summer, Ed Vard Grooter heard about another remarkable tulip that had been found in another garden, in another part of Holland. This tulip was red with bizarre, purple-speckled spackles. And Ed Vard knew at once that *it* was the most valuable flower in all the world.

"That tulip is worth at least a gaggle of ganders and a giggle of geese, eight snorting pigs and twelve shearable sheep; two bellowing bulls and a full cart of wheat," moaned Ed Vard Grooter. He was now more envious than ever.

A TALE *of* ONIONS

The moon and the cats were high in the masts and the piles of onions were low in the aft when Captain Zooter sailed away.

"Dag," cried Gretel Grooter. "Dag, so long, good-bye."

"*Boooooweeeeet!*" the bosun's whistle shrieked.

"*Meeeeeooooow!*" purred the cargo of cats.

The flute flew out of Oostende on a bluster of breeze and rounded the cape in two months and a half. Its bow pointed due east to the Indies, and it sped along on the briskest of seas. And Captain Drooter van Zooter ate his onions. He sat on the deck in the spray and the foam, with the tilt and the pitch and the bob and the roll, and devoured his piles and piles of onions.

They were closing in on Kracka-toe-Krack when the sky turned an ominous black. Suddenly, the wind began to howl and the sails began to snap. Captain Drooter van Zooter rolled aside his onions, rolled back his map, and groaned, "We're here. We're here. We're precisely here, we're precisely here at the dreaded spot. The spot where the Northerly-Southerly-Westerly-Easterly-Every-Which-Wherely blows."

And blow it did.

"We're going under," the bosun cried. "We've got to lighten the ship. This flute is full, and only

a fool would fail to fling out its load. Quick, take action, be bold! Pitch out the cargo of cats!"

"Never," thundered Captain Drooter van Zooter. "I'm a man of the sea, and I've given my word to carry this cargo of cats. Not just to here or to there or wherever you please, but all the way to Kracka-toe-Krack."

Then Captain Drooter van Zooter peered down into the aft and he knew what he had to do. He felt sick in his stomach and weak in his knees, but he yelled out to the crew, "Toss out the onions, toss out each and every one of them!"

FLORAES
MALLEWAGEN

A TALE *of* TULIPS

In early spring of the following year, just as he was selling his blooms, Ed Vard Grooter heard about still another remarkable tulip that had been found in still another garden, in still another part of Holland. This tulip was blue with bizarre, purple-speckled, spackled spickles. And Ed Vard knew at once that *it* was the most valuable flower in all the world.

"It's worth at least a gaggle of ganders and a giggle of geese, eight snorting pigs and twelve shearable sheep; two bellowing bulls and a full cart of wheat; a barrel of butter and a great poster bed for both snoring and sleep," moaned Ed Vard Grooter. He was now even more envious than ever.

A TALE *of* ONIONS

In her tower window sat Gretel Grooter, painting away and longing for her Captain Drooter. She stared out to sea at a distant mast, sniffed at an onion, and dreamt of the past. She sniffed at an onion, and sorrow filled her, but there was nary a sign of the *Gulden Guilder.*

A TALE *of* TULIPS

In the late spring of the following, following year, while walking amidst his blooming tulips, Ed Vard Grooter suddenly spotted it. There, right before his eyes, growing in his *very own* garden, was a truly remarkable tulip! It was bright yellow with bizarre, purple-speckled, spackled, spickled freckles. And Ed Vard knew at once that it was far and away the most valuable flower in all the world.

"Zounds!" cried Ed Vard Grooter. "Why, this tulip—my tulip—is worth at least a gaggle of ganders and a giggle of geese, eight snorting pigs and twelve shearable sheep; two bellowing bulls and a full cart of wheat; a barrel of butter and a great poster bed for both snoring and sleep; a round wheel of cheese and a large golden trunk full of hankies to sneeze." He was now as happy as he could possibly be. He was the happiest tulip-grower in the whole of Holland.

That high summer, when the weather was warmer and all the tulips had wilted, Ed Vard Grooter dug up his tulip bulb and placed it on a shiny silver tray for everyone to admire.

A TALE *of* TULIPS, A TALE *of* ONIONS

In the spring of the following, following, following year, Gretel Grooter finally gave up waiting for her Drooter van Zooter. She had turned from her window and was slamming the slats when suddenly she saw him stumbling up from the sea—covered from the top of his head to the tips of his toes in cats.

"It's my Drooter!" screamed Gretel Grooter. "His legs are wobbly, he's onion-skin thin—and I've—Oh, no, I've nothing cooked to welcome him! I've no onions stewed, no onions boiled, no onions baked, no onions fried. I've no onions with liver or cod. How odd that I should forget his onions. I must zip to the market like a Chinese rocket and buy my Drooter onions."

"Come in, dear Drooter," said Ed Vard Grooter to Captain Drooter van Zooter as Captain Drooter van Zooter stepped through the door. "I see you're home from the sea."

"Yes," said Captain Drooter van Zooter. "As you can see, I'm home from the sea, and I've got some tales not many can tell. I've sailed through whirling typhoons and howling gales. But the most horrible horror of all is that I've been without my onions."

Then Ed Vard held up his tulip bulb on the shiny silver tray and beamed, "As I see you're home from the sea, I've something amazing for you to see. It's bizarre. It's purple. It's speckled. It's spackled. It's spickled. It's freckled...."

"It's an ONION!" roared Captain Drooter van Zooter. A wild look came to his eyes, and he shook from his hair to his bunions. "Oh, I've been at sea for ever so long without the taste of an onion. An onion, an onion, an onion! I've got to taste that onion!"

Then, before Ed Vard Grooter could respond, or before he could even gasp, Captain Drooter van Zooter grabbed the tulip bulb, gobbled it down, made a face, and rasped, "My, that was a horrible-tasting onion!"

"My tulip bulb! My tulip bulb!" Ed Vard Grooter cried. "You've swallowed my precious tulip bulb. I can't believe my eyes. My tulip bulb! My tulip bulb!" Ed Vard Grooter screamed. "I'll tie a rope around your boots and hang you from a beam. I'll shake you, I'll rattle you and hope that it pops out. I'll quiver, quake, and quaver you and swing you all about. I've got to have my tulip back, of that I have no doubt!"

Just then, the door flew open, and Ed Vard's jaw dropped down. Into the house rushed Gretel Grooter, followed by all the folk in town—and everyone was carrying tulips.

"Father... Drooter!" cried Gretel Grooter. "I've just seen the most amazing thing. All the fields in the whole of Holland are aburst and blooming with remarkable tulips."

"Truly remarkable tulips!" cried all the folk in town. "White tulips with bizarre purple speckles; red tulips with bizarre, purple-speckled spackles; blue tulips with bizarre, purple-speckled, spackled spickles; and yellow tulips with bizarre, purple-speckled, spackled, spickled freckles."

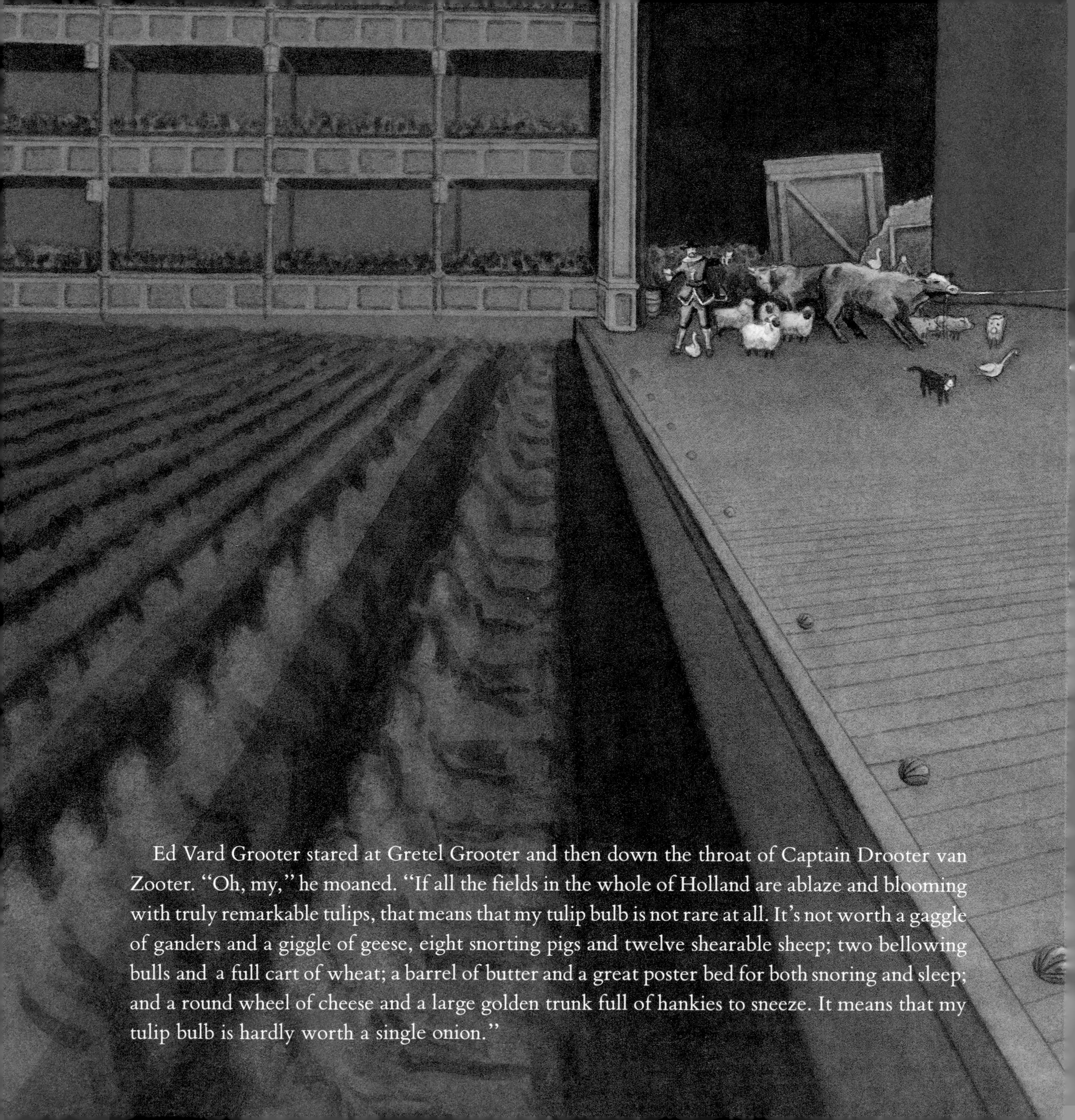

Ed Vard Grooter stared at Gretel Grooter and then down the throat of Captain Drooter van Zooter. "Oh, my," he moaned. "If all the fields in the whole of Holland are ablaze and blooming with truly remarkable tulips, that means that my tulip bulb is not rare at all. It's not worth a gaggle of ganders and a giggle of geese, eight snorting pigs and twelve shearable sheep; two bellowing bulls and a full cart of wheat; a barrel of butter and a great poster bed for both snoring and sleep; and a round wheel of cheese and a large golden trunk full of hankies to sneeze. It means that my tulip bulb is hardly worth a single onion."

"Onions," said Captain Drooter van Zooter, staring longingly at Gretel Grooter.
"Yes! Onions!" sighed Gretel Grooter, staring longingly at her Captain Drooter.

"Yes! Onions!" cried all the folk in town. "We'll stew them, we'll boil them, we'll bake them, we'll fry them, we'll serve them with liver and cod!"

And so they did.

THIS WAS A TALE OF TULIPS. THIS WAS A TALE OF ONIONS.
WAS IT ONE TALE OR TWO? WELL, THAT'S UP TO YOU.
WE SIMPLY DON'T HAVE AN OP-ONION.

A NOTE *to* YOUNG READERS

A Tale of Tulips, A Tale of Onions is based on the tulipomania craze that affected the country of Holland from 1634 to 1637. The seventeenth century was the golden age of buying and selling in Holland. During that time the country was governed by wealthy trading families, who built splendid houses in which to hang their splendid paintings.

Cargo ships called *flutes* sailed all about the world in search of things to buy and sell. Trading settlements were established in Africa, Indonesia (the Moluccan Islands), the New World and as far away as Japan. In order to handle all of their buying and selling, the people of Holland even established the first stock exchange.

While this fondness for buying and selling brought great wealth, it also brought on a great debacle known as the tulipomania craze. In the 1630s, a virus called *mosaic* began to infect the tulip bulbs of Holland. This virus caused the tulip petals to develop contrasting stripes, or *flames*. The Dutch called these infected tulip bulbs "bizarres." Popular taste dictated that the more bizarre the bizarres, the more valuable they were.

Slowly, tulipomania set in, and all the people of Holland began buying bizarre tulip bulbs. Nobles, farmers, seamen, footmen, maidservants—even chimney sweeps and old clothes-women—spent all they had on bizarre tulip bulbs. Everyone imagined that the great tulipomania would last forever; that the price of tulips would continue to rise, and that they would all become rich.

Some people, however, eventually decided to sell their bulbs. Soon, many others followed their example, and like a snowball rolling downhill, the selling accelerated. In a short time, nobody wanted to buy tulip bulbs anymore, and the price of tulip bulbs fell to where a tulip bulb was worth no more than a common onion.